Turtle's Penguin Day

valeri gorbachev

Alfred A. Knopf

New York

One night, Father Turtle read Little Turtle
a story about penguins.

When Little Turtle fell asleep, he dreamed he was a penguin. He played on the ice and dove into the water and swam and splashed with the other penguins.

In the morning, Little Turtle decided he wanted to be a penguin. He put on his red slippers and waddled from side to side. After breakfast, Little Turtle had an idea. He went up to the attic and found his grandfather's black jacket in an old chest, and he put it on.

"Now I look like a real penguin," said Little Turtle, staring at himself in the mirror.

"Hurry up, honey," said Mother Turtle.
"Or you'll be late for school."
"I'm ready," said Little Turtle.

"You can't go to school in that funny costume!" said Mother Turtle.

"It's not a funny costume," said Little Turtle. "I'm a penguin!" And then he put the book about penguins into his backpack and waddled outside to the school bus.

"Hello, Little Turtle," called the kids
on the school bus. "Great costume!"

"Thank you," said Little Turtle.
"I'm a penguin from the South Pole."

"Ms. Dog, look!" cried the children when they got to school. "We have a penguin in our class!"

"Oh my!" said Ms. Dog. "Why do you look like a penguin today, Little Turtle?"

"Because Daddy read me this
book about penguins last night,"
said Little Turtle. "I love penguins."

"I love waddling from side to side like penguins do."

"I love sliding on my belly like penguins do."

"I even love to sleep standing up like penguins do!" said Little Turtle.

"We want to be penguins too!" cried all the children. So while Ms. Dog read to them from the penguin book, they all tried to pass balls to each other using just their feet, the way penguins do with their eggs.

And when they had recess, Little Turtle and
his friends slid down the slide on their bellies,
pretending they were penguins sliding on the ice.

During music time, they all danced a waddling penguin dance.

And at nap time, all of them dreamed penguin dreams.

"How was school today?" asked Mother Turtle when Little Turtle came home.

"We had a penguin day," said Little Turtle. "It was great!"

That night, Little Turtle ate fish-shaped crackers with dinner because penguins love fish.

And before he went to sleep, Little Turtle brushed his penguin beak.

Even when Little Turtle got into bed,
he still pretended to be diving and
swimming with his penguin friends.

Then Father Turtle brought a new bedtime
story to read.

"This is the story of a little monkey who lives
in a beautiful jungle," he said.

"Really?" said Little Turtle. "A monkey?"

And when Little Turtle fell asleep that night,
he dreamed he was a funny little monkey. . . .

THIS IS A BORZOI BOOK PUBLISHED BY ALFRED A. KNOPF

Copyright © 2008 by Valeri Gorbachev

All rights reserved. Published in the United States by Alfred A. Knopf, an imprint of Random House Children's Books, a division of Random House, Inc., New York.

Knopf, Borzoi Books, and the colophon are registered trademarks of Random House, Inc.

Visit us on the Web! www.randomhouse.com/kids

Educators and librarians, for a variety of teaching tools, visit us at www.randomhouse.com/teachers

Library of Congress Cataloging-in-Publication Data
Gorbachev, Valeri.
Turtle's penguin day / by Valeri Gorbachev.
p. cm.
Summary: After hearing a bedtime story about penguins, Turtle dresses as a penguin for school and soon the entire class is having a penguin day.
ISBN 978-0-375-84374-7 (trade) — ISBN 978-0-375-94564-9 (lib. bdg.)
[1. Turtles—Fiction. 2. Penguins—Fiction. 3. Schools—Fiction.] I. Title.
PZ7.G6475Tur 2008   [E]—dc22   2007037078

The text of this book is set in 20-point Seria.
The illustrations in this book were created using watercolors.

MANUFACTURED IN CHINA
August 2008
10 9 8 7 6 5 4 3 2 1
First Edition

Penguin Facts

- Penguins are birds, though unlike most birds, penguins can't fly. But they do swim, and they can hold their breath for a long time.

- When they are walking on land, penguins' short legs, which are positioned far back on their bodies, give them their funny waddle.

- Penguins are found only in the Southern Hemisphere. Most penguins live in Antarctica, near the South Pole.

- But not all penguins live in the cold—they can be found on hot tropical coasts, too! Galápagos penguins live on the Galápagos Islands, near the equator.

- They are warm-blooded animals—feathers and a layer of fat called blubber help protect them from the icy water. They also huddle together in big groups to help each other stay warm.

- Female penguins lay one or two eggs at a time. They usually build a nest of rocks, sticks, or grass, or they burrow underground.

- Penguin mothers and fathers take turns looking after the eggs and raising the chicks. While one parent looks after the eggs, the other parent goes to the ocean to eat. Emperor penguins and king penguins, who live in the cold Antarctic, hold their eggs, and later their chicks, on their feet to keep them warm.

- Penguins eat fish, squid, and tiny shrimplike animals called krill.

- Penguins love to play—they enjoy diving, surfing on the waves, and tobogganing through the ice and snow on their bellies.

- There are seventeen species of penguins. They come in all sorts of shapes and sizes. The emperor penguin is the largest and can weigh up to ninety pounds, while the smallest species is the little penguin—also known as the blue or fairy penguin—which weighs only two pounds.